WHAT WILL I DO WITH MY LOVE TODAY?

KRISTIN CHENOWETH

Illustrated by
Maine Diaz

An Imprint of Thomas Nelson

What Will I Do with My Love Today?

© 2022 Kristin Chenoweth

Tommy Nelson, PO Box 141000, Nashville, TN 37214

Published in Nashville, Tennessee, by Tommy Nelson. Tommy Nelson is an imprint of Thomas Nelson. Thomas Nelson is a registered trademark of HarperCollins Christian Publishing, Inc.

Tommy Nelson titles may be purchased in bulk for educational, business, fund-raising, or sales promotional use. For information, please email SpecialMarkets@ThomasNelson.com.

ISBN 978-1-4002-2845-4 (eBook)
ISBN 978-1-4002-2843-0 (HC)

Library of Congress Cataloging-in-Publication Data

Names: Chenoweth, Kristin, author. | Diaz, Maine, illustrator.
Title: What will I do with my love today? / Kristin Chenoweth; illustrated by Maine Diaz.
Description: Nashville, Tennessee, USA: Tommy Nelson, [2021] | Audience: Ages 4–8. | Summary: Illustrations and rhyming text follow a young girl experiencing the joy of adopting a dog.
Identifiers: LCCN 2021021215 (print) | LCCN 2021021216 (ebook) | ISBN 9781400228430 (hc) | ISBN 9781400228454 (ebook)
Subjects: CYAC: Stories in rhyme. | Dogs—Fiction. | Adoption—Fiction. | Pet adoption—Fiction. | Love—Fiction. | LCGFT: Picture books. | Stories in rhyme.
Classification: LCC PZ8.3.C4252 Wh 2021 (print) | LCC PZ8.3.C4252 (ebook) | DDC [E]—dc23
LC record available at https://lccn.loc.gov/2021021215
LC ebook record available at https://lccn.loc.gov/2021021216

Illustrated by Maine Diaz

Printed in Thailand

22 23 24 25 26 IMG 10 9 8 7 6 5 4 3 2 1

Mfr: IMG / Chachoengsao, Thailand / February 2022 / PO #12040408

To my Thunderpup, and to all the furry babies everywhere who show us how to love unconditionally day by day.

Every morning I wake up and say,

"What will I do with my love today?"

My heart's full of **love**.
I have so much to spare,
and all of God's creatures
need **KINDNESS** and **CARE**.

One Sunday morning,

I sang with the choir,

songs about love

lifting **higher**

and **HIGHER**.

We went out for ice cream,

and when I got mine,

Dad paid for the next person

standing in line.

I helped out my neighbor by pulling up weeds
to prepare her new garden
for all kinds of seeds.

While we got groceries, I sang Mom a song.

"You are my sunshine!" my dad sang along.

When we got to the chorus, a boy stacking beans

started dancing with girls buying ripe nectarines.

I heard a high note from somewhere near the spinach.

My teacher, Miss Bird, gave a big **Broadway** finish!

I gave her a hug, and my mom said, "See that?

Sing your **love** to the world, and more **love** will come back."

Sure enough, Mom was right!

When I checked in my heart,

I found **even more love**

than I had at the start!

I wanted to share it. I needed a way.

Then I saw a big sign . . .

I saw a sweet puppy

whose big, funny feet

made a **thunderous** noise

as she ran up to me.

Puppy hugs! Puppy kisses!

Such tail-wagging wiggles!

"Hello, Thunderpup!"

I said in between giggles.

"You're my pup!"

You're my person!

"We're made for each other!"

I hugged her and told her that I'd always love her.

Mom and Dad signed some papers
with lots of big words

to make it official:

she's mine, and I'm hers.

We skipped down the sidewalk and played at the park,

ate dinner and headed home just before dark.

The afternoon sun turned to rain clouds and lightning, and poor little Thunderpup found it so *frightening*.

She trembled and whimpered.

She jumped in my bed

and pulled up the blankets

to cover her head.

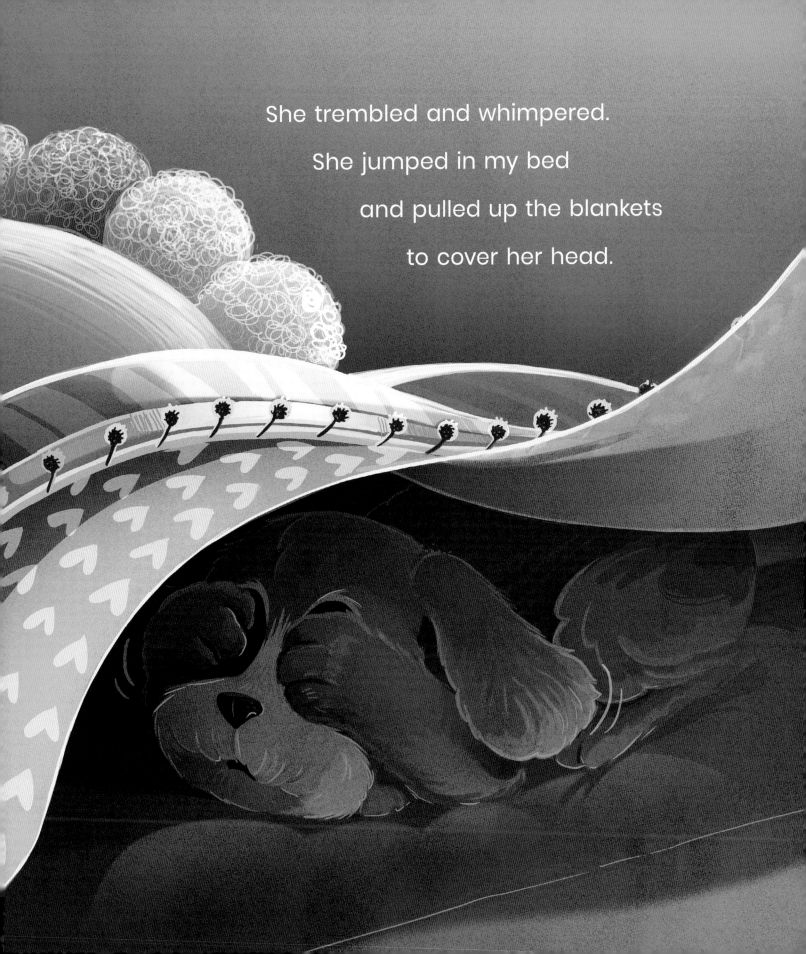

I crawled in beside her and gave her a hug.

"I got you," I said. "Don't be scared, Thunderpup.

When I was a baby
no bigger than you,
my mommy and daddy
adopted me too."

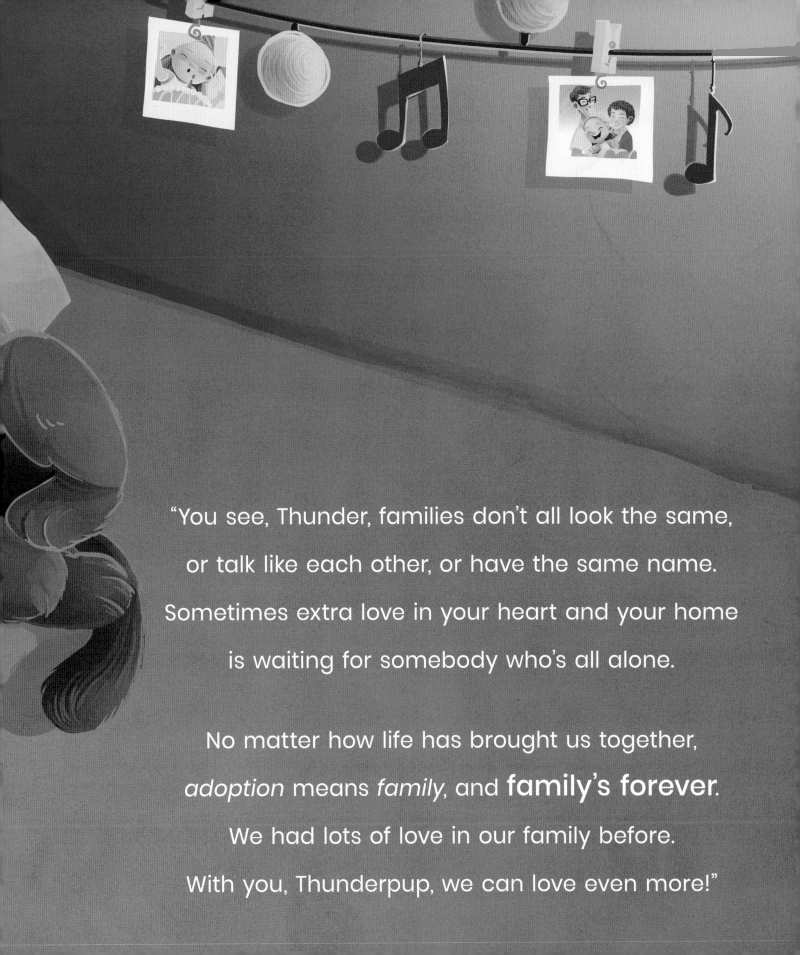

"You see, Thunder, families don't all look the same,
or talk like each other, or have the same name.
Sometimes extra love in your heart and your home
is waiting for somebody who's all alone.

No matter how life has brought us together,
adoption means *family*, and **family's forever**.
We had lots of love in our family before.
With you, Thunderpup, we can love even more!"

With Thunderpup helping,

I started to find

a lot of new ways

to be **CARING** and **KIND**.

She helped clear the table

while I did the dishes

and made sidewalk art with

pawprints and **tail swishes**.

I showed her the garden where I planted seeds.

"The rain helped them blossom!" I said. "**Look at these!**

Marigolds! Daffodils! Violets of blue!"

We decided to take some to Miss Bird at school.

Sharing love is like planting a seed that will grow much wilder and stronger than you'll ever know.

The more love you give,
the more love there will be.

Love as much as you can every day and you'll see.

That's exactly what Thunder
and I like to do.
Look! We put lots of love
here—in this book—for **YOU!**

So **give flowers** to friends and **sing songs** on the street. Find a way to bring joy to each person you meet!

Jump out of bed
every morning
and say . . .

"What will I do
with **my love** today?"